STAR
The Surprise

Home Farm Twins

Star

The Surprise

Jenny Oldfield

Illustrated by Kate Aldous

**Hodder
Children's
Books**

a division of Hodder Headline Limited

For Margaret and Autumn

A Catalogue record for this book is available from the British Library

ISBN 0 340 72798 5

Typeset by Avon Dataset Ltd, Bidford-on-Avon, Warks

Printed and bound in Great Britain by
The Guernsey Press Co. Ltd, Guernsey, Channel Isles

Hodder Children's Books
a division of Hodder Headline Limited
338 Euston Road
London NW1 3BH

One

'There's a new girl at school,' Helen Moore told her mum.

'Mmm.' Mary stared dreamily out of the kitchen window at the sunny, windswept daffodils on Doveton Fell.

'She's called Polly Moone.' Helen was on her way to join her twin sister, Hannah, in the barn. The girls planned to give their pony, Solo, a special Easter grooming; brush, wisp, sponge, hoof-oil; the lot.

Mary Moore followed her across the yard. 'Hmm. Just look up the hill, Helen: that's what Wordsworth meant by "A host of golden daffodils!"'

Helen walked on and dumped a bucket of warm,

1

soapy water inside Solo's stall. Then she chucked Hannah a sponge. 'Painful Polly's in our class, worse luck.'

'That's nice, dear.'

'"Nice"!' Helen mimed at Hannah, sticking two fingers in her mouth and making a sick face.

Hannah giggled and took up the tale. 'The Moones have moved into Manor Farm; you know, that old place off the main road, behind Doveton Manor.'

'Oh yes, lovely!'

'It's not lovely, it's a dump!' Helen protested. She knew the dismal house overlooking the lake. It had been empty for years and was practically falling down.

'*Was* a dump, is now stunning!' David Moore popped up from behind Solo, who stood patiently in the stall, loving all the attention. The grey pony's eyes were half-closed, his breathing deep and contented as David and Hannah brushed and rubbed. 'Major work has been done over the winter, money no object,' David reported with an envious sigh. 'New roof, new windows; everything. They've done up the old stable block too, apparently.'

'Great!' Standing by the barn door, the twins' mum still wasn't paying attention. She'd taken a rare day off from running the Curlew Cafe in Nesfield, and wanted to enjoy every drop of spring sunshine.

'Yeah!' Helen scoffed. 'Polly keeps going on and on about their twelve brilliant stables; like we care!'

Hannah took a comb and began work on Solo's white mane. 'She does go on a bit,' she agreed. 'Holly this, Holly that!'

'Who's Holly?' David grunted. He bent to pick out stones from Solo's hooves.

'Polly's horse,' Helen told him. 'She's won hundreds of rosettes for dressage, thousands of prizes for show-jumping, blah-blah-blah!'

'Holly-Polly, Polly-Holly!' Hannah laughed.

'Hmm.' At last Mary tuned in. She raised her eyebrows and studied her two dark-haired, brown-eyed daughters. 'Do I detect an anti-Polly Moone movement in the ranks? Could it be that my darling sweet girls don't like the newcomer at Manor Farm?'

'Well!' Hannah blushed, then ducked out of sight behind Solo.

'So?' Helen stood her ground. 'What's to like?'

'Helen!' David and Mary said together.

'Sorry,' she mumbled.

'. . . But it's true!' Helen whispered later, when their mum and dad had wandered off up the fell together.

She waited until they were out of earshot. 'Polly-Holly-Dolly Moone is a pain in the . . .'

'Helen!' Hannah dug her in the ribs.

'She is! She's a . . .'

'Forget it, OK!' Hannah called Speckle across the farmyard. 'Come on, I'll race you up the hill.'

'Get Sunny to look at the camera!' David Moore instructed. He'd squatted down on his haunches, with his lens only an arm's length from his subject. 'Come on, Hannah, get a grip!'

Hannah wrapped her arm firmly around Sunny's fat pink waist. The little pig squirmed and squealed, then wriggled backwards and escaped across the farmyard. 'Looks like he doesn't want to have his picture taken!' she gasped.

It was the afternoon of the golden daffodil walk, two days after Easter. Mary Moore sat in her regular spot on a cane chair under the chestnut tree, her feet up, taking in the sun.

'Catch him, Helen!' David cried.

Helen leaped down from the wall where she'd been whittling a stick with an old penknife. She dropped it and gave chase as Sunny scooted under Mary's legs, round the back of the tree.

'I'll never get this project finished in time,' David groaned. He made his living as a freelance photographer, taking pictures of animals for newspapers and magazines. 'It's a big job for one of the best country-life quarterlies. They're calling it "Living the Dream"!'

'Some dream!' Hannah muttered. She watched Helen fling herself headlong on top of the runaway pig. 'Slave labour, more like!'

'Well done, Helen!' Mary smiled and clapped.

'What now?' Helen held tight to a still-struggling Sunny.

'Bribe him to have his photo taken,' Mary winked.

'I've got to get a good picture,' David cried in a strained voice. 'Bring him back over here, quick.'

'But he won't sit still!' Taking the fat little pig from Helen, Hannah tried to pose for the camera again. She saw Helen creep behind their dad's back and heard her rustle something in her pocket. Suddenly Sunny stopped squirming.

'Pig-pig-pig!' Helen sang quietly, holding up a chocolate biscuit for Sunny to see.

'Good! That's better!' David crouched down, camera at the ready.

Nestling quietly in Hannah's arms, Sunny tilted his

head to one side, floppy ears suddenly pricked. He stretched his mouth as if he was smiling.

Click-click-click. 'Perfect!' David breathed. 'OK, Hann, you can let him go now.'

With aching arms she did as she was told. Sunny jumped down and sprinted for the biscuit, almost skittling David as he charged. He snaffled it from Helen's hand and chomped happily.

David's camera whirred as the film wound on. He eased himself upright with a low moan. 'There must be an easier way to earn money!' he complained to Mary.

As Helen and Hannah rewarded their pet for having his photograph taken like a good little pig, they overheard snatches of conversation between their mum and dad.

'Take the Moones at Manor Farm,' David muttered. 'They must have spent thousands on that place to get it up and running. And what does Richard Moone do for a living?'

'I guess he doesn't take photographs?' Mary said wryly, making room for David on her chair.

'According to the gossip Luke Martin hears in the village shop, he's an estate agent!'

'*That's* why they could afford to do all that work to the place and set it up as a riding school.'

Overhearing this, Helen's face developed a deep frown. 'You hear that? Polly-Holly-Dolly Moone lives at a riding school!' she hissed. Now she felt jealous of the pale, round-faced girl who'd come to sit at the desk next to her and who spent every playtime boasting about her chestnut thoroughbred. She wasn't proud of the way she felt, but she couldn't seem to help it.

'And livery stables,' David Moore was adding. 'Looking after other people's horses means they'll soon be raking money in . . . not like us, eh?'

'Fancy living with all those horses!' Hannah whispered enviously. She scratched Sunny's hairy pink back and watched his curly tail twitch.

'Yeah, but no pigs, I bet!' Helen looked on the bright side. She glanced round the yard at Speckle and Socks. 'And no dog or cat.'

'Maybe.' Hannah pointed out that most people round here had normal pets like cats, dogs and hamsters.

'OK then; no chickens and geese.' Helen pointed to the poultry pecking at grain by the stone trough. 'No goat, no donkey . . .' She began to reel off all the animals they'd given a home to here at Home Farm.

'But loads of horses!' Hannah cut in.

Helen bit her lip and fell silent. She let Sunny poke his blunt snout into her pocket to look for more chocolate biscuits. 'Hann, you don't think . . . ?'

Hannah frowned thoughtfully. '. . . That maybe we could . . .'

'I mean, just if we happen to be passing tomorrow when we meet Laura and ride Solo and Sultan by the lake. . .' Privately Helen considered the various possibilities.

Hannah nodded. She admitted to herself but not to Helen that she was curious about the posh new set-up at Manor Farm. 'And we might just *happen* to go in that direction . . . I mean, not on purpose, of course.'

'Yeah!' Helen shrugged. She patted Sunny then picked him up, feeling his warm, squidgy body cuddle up against her. 'Like, we'll probably ride pretty close by.'

'And take a look.'

'Without making it obvious.'

'Oh yeah. Without looking as if we'd planned to visit,' Hannah agreed. 'Tomorrow morning, then!'

The twins didn't want Polly Moone to have the least suspicion that they were interested in her and her precious horse. Or her precious stables. Or her riding school. No way!

Two

'*Yee-owwl*!' Lady, the Saunders' pencil-thin Siamese cat, paraded around the edge of the fish pond at Doveton Manor. She howled at Hannah as she rode Solo up the wide drive, with Helen pedalling slowly behind.

'Hi, Lady.' Hannah dismounted and looked around. 'Where's Laura got to?'

'*Yee-oww-owwl*!' The fashion-model cat put one elegant paw after another and whisked her long tail. She swept off along the stone patio, through french windows into the grand house.

'Ask a silly question . . .' Helen muttered. She dumped the bike and ran round the side of the manor into the stableyard.

Leading Solo, Hannah followed more slowly. 'It wasn't a silly question,' she protested. 'We've been waiting ten whole minutes for Laura at the end of the drive. I want to know where she is!'

'Laura?' Helen poked her head over the nearest stable door, which happened to belong to their friend's horse, Sultan. The thoroughbred was inside, all tacked up and ready to go, but with no sign of his rider. 'Where is she?' Helen murmured, taking in the horse's polished leather saddle and smart plaited reins.

'Huh!' Hannah scoffed. 'You're expecting a more sensible answer out of Sultan than out of Lady, are you?'

The big chestnut came to the door and poked out his head. His dark mane swished as he twisted his neck towards the house and let out a loud whinny. The sound of his voice brought a tall, slim figure to the french windows.

'Yeah!' Helen grinned at Hannah, turned and ran towards the house, meeting Laura Saunders halfway. 'What kept you?' she demanded, noting the fair-haired girl's glum expression.

'Sorry I'm late.' Laura flicked at her long leather boots with the end of her riding crop as she strode across the patio. 'Guess what my dad just did,' she muttered.

'Flew to the moon? Won the lottery?' Helen took wild guesses, but got no response. 'Hey, really, Laura, what's the matter?'

'Is it something to do with Sultan?' Hannah gathered that there was a serious reason behind Laura failing to show up at the gate.

'Yes and no.' Grim-faced, Laura led Sultan into the yard and together she and Hannah mounted. 'He's rented out some of our pastureland down by the lake. It's Sultan's favourite field!'

'Right!' Helen picked up her bike. She knew which patch of ground Laura meant. It was smooth and green, sprinkled at this time of year with yellow, blue and pink wild flowers, surrounded on three sides by neatly kept Lakeland stone walls. A narrow stream ran through it, then across the pebble shore to the clear, deep lake. She thought of their own small, tussocky paddock at Home Farm. 'But Sultan still has plenty of grazing closer to the house. You don't exactly need all this land to keep one solitary horse, do you?'

'That's not the point.' Still sulking, Laura pointed Sultan in the direction of the field they were talking about. She led the twins across the yard and down a bridleway leading to the lake.

'So who did your dad rent the land to?' Hannah asked. But the answer was already forming in her head. 'Don't tell me; it was to the Moones at Manor Farm!'

Laura looked sharply at her. 'How did you know?'

'Guesswork,' Hannah mumbled.

Helen overtook the two horses and cycled ahead. 'So what does Mr Moone want the extra pasture for?' she called over her shoulder. 'For the riding-school horses, I expect!'

'No.' Laura's frown deepened as they came within sight of the lakeside field. 'He wants it for his precious daughter, Polly, who I just met the other day, and that drop-dead gorgeous horse she's always going on about!'

'She is!' Hannah had to admit as she gazed across the rented field to where a chestnut horse almost as graceful as Sultan himself quietly grazed. 'Drop-dead gorgeous, I mean!'

Holly's coat was as glossy and brown as a new horse chestnut. She had four neat white socks and a white blaze running the length of her graceful face. Over fifteen hands high, she was powerfully built and obviously quite a handful for an eleven-year-old rider.

'Not as gorgeous as you, Sultan.' Laura leaned forward to pet her own thoroughbred's neck.

'Or you, Solo!' Hannah spoke up loyally for their own dappled grey pony. Twelve hands of solid, sturdy muscle, with not a drop of good breeding in him; to Helen and Hannah he was still the most beautiful, the most good natured, the most friendly and loyal horse on earth.

The girls fell silent as the horse in the field heard them and looked up. She started towards them in a pleasant, self-assured way, like a well-mannered hostess greeting guests at a party. *Hello. Welcome. How do you like my new apartment?* Reaching the wall where they stood, she tossed her elegant head and swished her silky, light-brown mane, indicating the lush pasture which she'd just moved into.

'Hello.' Helen stretched out a hand to let the mare nuzzle her empty palm. Then, smiling and talking gently, she rubbed the white stripe on her nose. Holly responded with a friendly lick of her jacket sleeve.

From up in the saddle, Hannah frowned and turned Solo away. Laura too sniffed and eased Sultan on along the bridleway. They were well on the way towards the lake, planning to walk the horses quietly along the pebbly beach past Manor Farm when Helen eventually grabbed her bike and caught them up.

A silence met her. Laura and Hannah rode on with only the hollow sound of hooves on stones, the slip and slide as metal shoes crunched over smooth pebbles.

'. . . Well!' Helen protested, struggling to keep up.

'Well what?' Hannah let her sister know that she'd been way too friendly with the rival horse.

'Holly's OK,' came the breathless protest. 'She can't help her owner, can she?'

They had no time to develop the argument. Up ahead lay the restored farmhouse recently occupied by the Moone family. It was time for the three girls to concentrate on looking casual while taking in the whole new set-up.

The first thing they saw was the house itself; a rambling old building with many pointed gables. A stone barn had been converted into extra living space by putting in a huge window where the double doors used to be. Laura stared hard at the conversion. 'That's an indoor swimming-pool!' she hissed.

'Their own private pool!' Hannah gasped, stopping to stare.

'Yeah, and look at the stables!' Helen pointed across a neat yard to a low, long building with a row of freshly-painted white doors. She counted six down one side of the yard, then six down a second side. And each stable was occupied. Grey horses, brown ponies, piebald Shetlands and black Welsh cobs waited attentively at the stable doors, tacked up and ready to be ridden.

'A class must be about to start,' Laura said, a few moments before a group of people in hard hats and jodhpurs appeared in the yard. They were led by a slight, sandy-haired woman dressed in a padded waistcoat, who bustled from stable to stable, leading out horses and making sure that riders got safely into the saddle.

'That must be Polly's mum,' Hannah decided, though the new girl at school, who was plump with long, straight dark hair, looked nothing like the woman in charge of the riding class.

'Come on, they'll see us if we're not careful!' Helen remembered the plan to pass casually by.

But her warning came too late. There was someone already breaking away from the group in the yard and running down to the beach, her hair tied up in a ponytail, smartly dressed in a yellow polo shirt and black jodhpurs.

'Polly Moone!' Laura and Hannah gasped. They snatched at the reins, ready for a quick getaway.

'Hi, Helen!' Polly saw the nearest twin on Solo and sang out a greeting. The headcollar and leadrope in her hand told them she must be heading to the field to fetch Holly.

'I'm Hann . . .' Hannah began, then shrugged. *Oh, never mind*!

'Hi, Hannah!' Polly said to Helen, rushing on. 'Hi, Laura!'

'Hi!' they mumbled back, their faces red, looking anywhere except in Polly's direction.

'Come on!' Helen said through gritted teeth. She wheeled her battered bike across the pebbles, feeling as if she'd been caught doing something really bad. 'Let's get out of here!'

'No, wait!' Hannah had turned for one last glance at the stableyard. She'd spotted a familiar figure. Her mouth fell open as she let Solo's reins hang loose and watched a man with a camera in earnest conversation with the sandy-haired woman.

Frowning, Helen looked up across the beach. The

man was nodding and shaking hands with Polly's mum. His wavy hair was ruffled by the breeze, his black camera bag on the ground beside him. 'Dad!' she gasped.

'What's *he* doing here?' Laura asked. Sultan jumped and skittered sideways at the sharp sound of her voice.

'Excuse me!' Polly interrupted. She had all the room in the world to pass with Holly on the leadrope, but she made a big show of squeezing by. The beautiful horse tossed her mane again and held her head high.

'That's our dad!' Helen exclaimed, her mouth still open. 'Why? What? I mean . . . How come?'

'He's working here, didn't you know?' Polly smiled sweetly. She paused to let Holly say hello to Sultan and Solo.

It was Hannah's turn to let her jaw drop. 'You mean, mucking-out type work?'

'No, silly!' Polly laughed. 'I mean taking photographs type work. I heard him ask Mum if he could take pictures of Manor Farm and the horses.'

'What for!' Helen could still hardly believe her eyes. Yet there was their dad, camera in position, taking close-ups of the horses against the backdrop of the newly renovated farmhouse. *Click-click-click*; like he did.

'For a country magazine,' Polly explained as she led Holly on towards the house. 'Photos for an article called "Living the Dream", I think. Mum said to go ahead and take all the shots he needs!'

Click-click. Wonderful! Great! Thank you very much!

Three

'What a traitor!' Laura hissed when she understood what the twins' dad was up to. A deep frown creased her forehead.

'I wouldn't go that far,' Helen objected.

'He must have a good reason to be taking pictures of Manor Farm.' Hannah coped with her surprise and came over all reasonable. She wanted to stand up for her father.

But Laura shook her head and began to ride on, muttering as she went. 'I don't see why he has to go and make friends with the Moones of all people.'

Hannah pulled a face at Helen, showing her teeth and dragging down the corners of her mouth. 'What now?'

Jenny Oldfield

Helen shrugged. She saw that Polly Moone and Holly had reached the yard and that Mrs Moone was quickly saddling the horse. Their dad was still busily taking photos.

'Are you two coming, or what?' Laura shouted over her shoulder. She began to trot Sultan through the shallow water at the edge of the lake. The proud chestnut kicked up spray and surged on.

'Er – no!' Hannah had given in to temptation. The urge to join their dad had won, and she reined Solo towards the farm.

'See you later!' Helen yelled. After all, it was only natural to want to talk to your dad. It still didn't mean they were ready to make friends with Polly-Holly-Dolly Moone.

Dolly suited her, she decided, drawing close to the stableyard and glancing up at the group of riders ready to set out on a hack through the Lakeland countryside. Polly was at the front. Her hard hat hid her long, black hair but couldn't disguise the doll-like features; the big, clear grey eyes with long dark lashes, the snub-nose, the little rosebud mouth.

With a sharp kick against Holly's sides, Polly began the ride. She smiled sweetly at the twins as she passed by, setting off in the same direction as Laura and

24

Sultan. Then David turned and spotted them and he hauled them across the yard to meet Linda Moone.

'And these are the new stables!' David explained after the introductions. He waved his arm towards the best equipped, airiest, cleanest horse accommodation Helen and Hannah had ever seen.

'Tack-room over here.' He led them with a smiling Mrs Moone to a well-organised store where new bridles hung in a neat row. There were shelves full of grooming equipment, rows of hard hats, spare saddles, piles of rugs, a big first-aid kit and a stack of rakes and brushes used for mucking out. 'I knew you'd be impressed!' he grinned.

'If only we had half of this stuff for you, Solo!' Hannah murmured, still keeping hold of the pony's reins.

'Dream on!' Helen sighed. She heard a phone ring from inside the house and turned to her dad as Mrs Moone rushed to answer it. 'Unreal!' she gasped.

'Not jealous, are you?' he quizzed. He checked the number of shots left on his film and motioned for Helen and Hannah to follow him out of the tack-room across the yard.

'No!' they both shot back. Then they sighed. 'Yes!' they admitted.

'Don't be.' David paused for a serious talk in the spring sunshine. 'The Moones are just like us, except they have money.'

'Like us?' Helen echoed.

'No way!' Hannah scoffed.

'Yes. They like living in the country – we do too. They've moved out of the city into an old farm, like we did. And they love horses . . .'

'Like we do!' Hannah and Helen chimed in. Their dad was quickly winning them over. Hannah even said she was sure she and Solo, Socks, Speckle, Sunny and all the rest of the animals at Home Farm could soon get used to the plush lifestyle here at Manor Farm. And Helen grudgingly admitted that a morning swim in your own private pool on a sunny day like today would be like having a slice of heaven.

'So would you like to see one more very special thing?' David asked, obviously happy to have converted them.

'What?' Hannah tethered Solo to an iron ring fixed into a nearby stone wall.

'Where?' Helen had already ditched the bike and was following eagerly.

'In here.' Getting his camera ready, their dad led them into the last stable in the row.

26

It was spacious and light, with white-painted walls.
The floor was covered by a thick layer of fresh wood
shavings; less dusty than straw but a more expensive
form of bedding, as Helen and Hannah knew. And
there, standing quietly, attentively watching her
visitors, stood a dapple grey mare. Fifteen hands high,
with a darker mane and tail, her swollen belly showed
that she'd reached the late stage of pregnancy.

'Meet Lady Jane Grey,' David Moore said, raising his
camera to take close-up shots of the mother-to-be.

'Oh, gorgeous!' Hannah breathed. She held back
so as not to disturb the mare.

'Or what!' Helen murmured. The horse's dark eyes looked enormous in her pale grey face. Her face was long and straight, her neck arched, her limbs long and slender; sure signs that this was a well-bred, valuable mare. 'Now I really *am* jealous of Polly Moone. As if one chestnut thoroughbred wasn't enough!'

'No need.' David altered the focus on his camera lens. 'Lady Jane's in livery here. She doesn't belong to the Moones.'

'Who then?' Hannah edged forward. She reached out her hand and softly stroked the mare's dappled neck.

'She belongs to William Baxter, a friend of ours who lives in North Yorkshire.' Linda Moone had just returned from the house and overheard the last few sentences. 'Lady Jane is in livery with us until she produces her foal, which we reckon should be in about three weeks' time.'

'And what's her background?' David took a notepad and pen from his pocket, ready to make notes. 'I need the information for the caption underneath her photo if it's chosen for the magazine article,' he explained.

'Well, it's a very good blood line, actually.' Linda leaned on the stable door, hands clasped. 'Her sire is

Desert Bloom, out of Queen Margaret; both top-grade thoroughbreds. Lady Jane here was sent to stud with Caramel Cream, over at Malton near York. He's produced three or four very good steeplechasers in his time; Harry Hotspur and Walnut Whip amongst them.'

Helen grimaced at Hannah. The horses' fancy names conjured up a peculiar mixture of royalty and chocolate. But she'd been right; Lady Jane Grey was worth a whole heap of money.

Hannah felt the mare's soft nose nuzzle her palm. Thoroughbred or not, Lady Jane was just like any other horse when it came to looking for treats.

'Here, give her a Polo mint.' Linda sought in her pocket and handed the sweet to Helen, who passed it on to Hannah. The mare nipped it between her lips, tipped her head back and crunched it between her teeth.

'Manners!' Hannah reminded her. 'Say thank you!'

Lady Jane lowered her head and nudged Hannah's shoulder.

'That's better.' Helen smiled, then turned to see good old Solo poking his head over the stable door, barging Mrs Moone out of the way in his eagerness not to be left out. 'Hey, how did you get loose?'

Jenny Oldfield

Nudge, nudge; the grey pony shoved Linda Moone
sideways. He craned his head, nostrils flaring as he
picked up the delicious scent of Polo mint.

'Solo can smell "treat" a mile off!' David laughed,
turning to point the camera and take cute shots of
the twins' pony bullying the rich stable owner.

'Here!' Linda regained her balance and dug into
her pocket for another mint. 'A polo for Solo!'

Solo snaffled it greedily.

'Talking of manners . . .' The twins' dad grinned as
he finished off the film.

'Thank you!' Hannah and Helen chimed on Solo's
behalf, blushing and grinning too.

It was time to leave. But, as they gathered together
in the yard, while Helen mounted Solo for the
ride home and Hannah picked up the bike, Linda
Moone told them how nice their unexpected visit
had been.

'Drop in on us any time,' she insisted, shaking
hands with David once more, then turning to the
twins. 'Especially now that we know you girls are as
mad on horses as Polly is, feel free to visit.'

'Thanks,' Helen mumbled. Mention of Polly had
wiped the happy smile off her face. And, worse than
that, she thought she'd caught a glimpse of Laura and

Sultan hanging about by the lakeside, watching the twins' every move.

'I mean it!' Mrs Moone repeated the invitation. 'Come and see how Lady Jane is getting along. We're all very excited by the prospect of her having her foal here at Manor Farm while William's travelling abroad. He's put a lot of trust in us, considering we're a new business. So, if you've never seen a birth before, perhaps you'd like to be here when—'

'No thanks!' Helen cut in, sounding rude without meaning to. Yes, that definitely was Laura waiting for them on the beach. She made a sign to Hannah that they'd best be off as quickly as possible.

David shrugged at Linda. 'They're probably a bit squeamish about the idea,' he apologised.

'No, Dad, but we have to go!' Hannah picked up the signal. She too saw Laura and Sultan in the distance. 'Bye, Mrs Moone. Bye, Dad. See you back at Home Farm!'

'. . . Well, I can't tell you how pleased I am that Polly has made new friends so quickly,' Linda confided in David Moore as the girls hurried off. 'It's always such a worry when children move schools, don't you think? It must have been the same for the twins when you first came to Doveton, although of course Helen and Hannah always have each other . . .'

'Uh-ohh!' Hannah groaned, pedalling ahead of Helen and Solo. As they drew near to Laura, she could see the black looks their friend was giving them from the water's edge.

'Pretend nothing's wrong,' Helen suggested. She let Solo trot the last couple of hundred metres, overtaking Hannah before she pulled up close to a scowling Laura. 'Hi, how far did you get?' she asked breezily.

Laura tossed her head and sniffed.

'Dad got some good pictures back there,' Hannah said breathlessly. 'There's a mare called Lady Jane Grey who's about to have a foal . . .'

'Ttt!' Laura raised her eyebrows and turned Sultan away.

'Don't be like that!' Hannah pleaded. It was no use trying to pretend that things were OK; Laura was making it obvious that she was really mad. 'It's not like we went and made friends with Polly or anything!'

All she got by way of reply was the sight of Laura's straight, slim back and the up-down, up-down bob of her head as she urged Sultan into a trot.

'Go after her!' Hannah gasped at Helen.

So Helen and Solo set off gamely after the long-legged chestnut. 'Lady Jane and Holly aren't anything like as beautiful as Sultan!' Helen tried the most obvious method of making up with an angry Laura, but she found she was still talking to an unresponsive, stiff, silent back.

Laura trotted on, until suddenly she seemed to change her mind. She reined Sultan to a halt, then turned haughtily. 'It's obvious what you and Hannah are like!' she said, her eyes darting black looks as she struggled to hold her horse steady. Sultan was fighting for his head, his hooves clattering on the smooth pebbles. 'As soon as you get the chance, you suck up to someone new and dump your old friends. I know your type.'

'We didn't . . .' Helen protested.

'Laura, don't be like this!' Hannah begged.

'Like what? I don't know what you mean.' Finish. End of conversation. Laura gave in to Sultan. The high-spirited horse turned and launched into a full canter.

A dazed Hannah stared at a helpless Helen. '"Suck up"!' she repeated.

'"Dump"!' Helen echoed.

'What are we going to do now?' they whispered together.

Four

As things turned out, there was *nothing* to be done.

'What's wrong with you two?' Mary Moore asked, as the twins moped about the house that Sunday evening.

'Laura doesn't like us any more,' Hannah told her, hunched up on the window-seat with Socks curled in her lap.

'She thinks we've made friends with Polly because of Holly, but we haven't. Holly's great, of course, but we don't even like Polly!' Helen rushed in with her explanation.

'Whoa!' Her mum threw up both hands to make her slow down. When she heard about the argument at the lakeside, she shook her head sadly. 'If a person doesn't want to be friends any more, there isn't a lot you can do to make her.'

'Even if she has got the wrong end of the stick,' David confirmed.

'But we still like Laura!' Hannah sighed.

'And Sultan,' Helen added unnecessarily.

Mary sat by Hannah and Socks, then waited for Helen to join them. 'If you ask me, the problem here is a touch of jealousy on Laura's part.'

Hannah frowned. 'Who's she jealous of; us?'

'No, stupid! Not us: Polly!' Helen snapped, ignoring her mum's dark look. 'The Saunderses are rich, yes! But the Moones are even richer. They've got bigger, better stables, more horses . . . a swimming pool!'

'Who cares?' Hannah shook her head.

'Laura cares; that's who.'

'So what can we do?' Hannah came round full-circle.

'Nothing.' Mary smiled sadly. 'Wait a while. Give Laura a chance to come to terms with having the Moones as neighbours. Meanwhile, be nice to Polly at school. Remember, being the new kid is hard. Do your best to include her in things. Help her to settle in.'

* * *

'Holly jumped a five foot wall yesterday!' Polly Moone told Hannah. She leaned across Helen's desk during registration, while Miss Wesley called out the names on the alphabetical list. 'The day before that she jumped a ten foot water jump!'

'Great.' Hannah smiled and nodded.

'Sam Lawson!' Miss Wesley called.

'Yes, Miss!' The twins' neighbour from Crackpot Farm answered to his name.

'Kylie Leech!'

'Miss!'

'. . . Last Saturday, I entered Holly into the junior showjumping event in Appleby,' Polly gushed, pushing Helen's bag off her desk without even noticing. Her grey eyes were alight at the memory of her horse's latest moment of showjumping glory.

'Polly Moone!' Miss Wesley's voice sang out.

'. . . She came first, in front of Gwyneth Turner on Minty, who was last season's under-thirteen north west champion!' Polly's chest puffed out, her round face beamed.

'Great!' Hannah said faintly. This was Thursday; the fourth day running that Polly Moone had bored her silly with her horse stories. The twins' promise to

Mary to be nice to the boastful new girl was beginning to wear pretty thin. Helen had already given up, but Hannah was still doing her best.

'Polly Moone . . . ?' Miss Wesley repeated. 'Polly . . . ?'

Helen scrabbled on the floor to pick up her bag, then sat back in her chair grinning at Sam as the irritated teacher stood up and came quickly down the aisle.

'Polly, I've called your name three times now and you still haven't bothered to answer!'

'What? Oh, sorry, Miss! Here, Miss!' Polly blushed. As Miss Wesley went to sit down, she turned accusingly to Helen. 'You could've warned me!' she hissed.

Helen's grin faded and her jaw dropped. 'Me?'

'Yes, you!' To Polly it was clearly Helen's fault that she'd got into trouble.

'I would have if I could have got a word in edgeways!' Helen protested with an innocent, injured look.

But it made no difference; Miss Wesley called Hannah's name on the register, and Polly Moone turned round in her seat to collar Sam Lawson, and continued the next episode of Holly the Wonder Horse.

* * *

'Hello, Hannah, you look worn out!' David Moore greeted her on Friday afternoon as she trudged home through the farmyard. He carried a big blue folder of photographs under his arm; the latest additions to "Living the Dream", which he placed carefully on the back seat of the car.

'I am,' she sighed. 'I've had a whole week of Polly Moone.'

Her dad gave her a sympathetic smile. 'Where's Helen?'

'She ran ahead to call Laura. She wants to find out if she'll come riding with us after tea.' Knowing that their friend would be home from school for the weekend, Helen had thought it was a good idea to get in touch. Hannah had advised caution, but Helen had gone ahead and done it anyway. 'I can guess what the answer will be,' she sighed, swinging her school bag down from her shoulder and waiting in the warm afternoon sun for Helen to emerge from the house.

'No good?' David asked, pausing by the car and judging from the dejected look on Helen's face that Hannah had guessed right.

Helen shook her head. 'Laura's dad answered. He couldn't even get her to come to the phone and speak

39

to me! I knew from the way Mr Saunders was talking that Laura was there, but all I could do was leave a message.'

Just then the phone rang.

'Maybe she changed her mind.' As Helen dashed off, David crossed his fingers and gave Hannah a hopeful smile.

Inside the house, Helen grabbed the phone. 'Hi, Laura!' she gasped. 'Listen, I'm really glad you rang—'

'It's not Laura,' a girl's voice interrupted. 'It's Polly!'

'Oh!' Helen let her voice fall flat.

'Polly Moone; you know—'

'Yeah, yeah.' If this phone call was about Holly the Wonder Horse, Helen felt she would scream.

'Listen, Hannah . . .'

'Helen, actually.'

'Listen, Helen, can you or Hannah tell your dad to get down to Manor Farm right now?' Polly rushed on in a loud, excited voice.

'Dad? Now? What for?' Helen held the receiver away from her ear and turned with a puzzled look to Hannah standing in the doorway.

'It's Lady Jane Grey!' Polly shouted.

Hannah could hear the message from a couple of metres away.

'She's having her foal early!'

'You're joking!' Helen gasped into the phone.

'No, honestly, it's happening now, right this very minute! Your dad could get some amazing pictures if he hurries. You and Hannah come too. See you soon. Bye!'

'This is quite a surprise.' Linda Moone greeted David, Hannah and Helen as they piled out of the car in the stableyard at Manor Farm. She was dressed in a shirt and jeans, her sandy hair held back from her face by a red patterned bandana. 'We weren't expecting this foal to be born until late April or early May.'

'Am I too late to take photographs of the birth?' Quickly David Moore slung his camera round his neck and headed for Lady Jane Grey's stable.

'No, don't panic.' Mrs Moone stood to one side. 'She's still in the first stage of labour; contractions have started and she's sweating up, but there's no sign of her beginning to strain.' Looking at the twins' doubtful faces and picking up the reason for their reluctance, she smiled. 'Don't worry. It's not as gruesome as it sounds. Come and see!'

Hannah and Helen both swallowed hard. They felt that they'd been rushed into coming without having had time to think. Once Helen had passed on Polly's message to their dad, he'd whisked them into the car and down through the village, out to Manor Farm. Now here they were, half-excited and longing to see the birth, but also half-worried about letting Laura down. They returned Linda Moone's pleasant greeting with uneasy smiles, wondering what on earth their old friend would say when she found out that they'd been here.

'After you!' Helen told Hannah, hanging back.

'No, no; after you!' Hannah countered.

Polly Moone's dark head popped up over the stable door, her eyes wide, her voice dramatic. 'This is fantastic!' she hissed. 'Lady Jane's lying down now; she's starting to strain! Hurry up, you two, or you'll miss the best bit!'

Helen took a deep breath, Hannah bit her lip.

'Amazing!' their dad's voice said softly from inside the stable where the birth was happening. There was a pause while his camera clicked and whirred. 'Oh girls, come and take a look!'

'*You* first!' Hannah prodded Helen in the back.

Helen turned and grabbed Hannah's arm. 'Together!'

They stepped inside the warm, dry stable just

in time to see the foal being born.

She came out feet-first, the dark, wet head appearing soon after, still surrounded by the pale coloured birth sac. Meanwhile, Lady Jane lay on her side without moving, taking a break from the strain of giving birth and getting ready for the final push.

'Urghh!' Helen put a hand to her mouth and groaned. How had they got themselves into this, she wondered.

Hannah blinked and looked away.

'Good girl!' Polly had dropped to her knees in the bed of straw and was encouraging the mare to push again. She crouched behind her without flinching, in the best position to see the foal finally born.

'No complications, thank heavens.' Linda Moone stood and observed as David busily took pictures. 'Apart from the fact that the little rascal is early and has caught us by surprise, it looks like she's perfectly normal and healthy!'

As she spoke, the newborn creature slithered fully into sight. Polly took a handful of clean straw to wipe the nostrils. The foal shuddered and took her first breath.

'Ohh!' Hannah whispered. 'She's shaking her head.'

'Poor thing, she's shivering!' Helen crept closer.

'That's OK. She'll begin to get up soon.' Polly had

watched every move and now shuffled back to give Lady Jane space to turn and lick her foal clean.

Click! David got a close-up shot of the heads of mother and baby. 'Perfect!' he murmured.

'She's trying to stand!' Helen could hardly believe that the tiny foal would have the strength. And no; she had struggled to her knees but now she was down in the straw again.

'Ahh!' Hannah groaned. She clenched her hands and willed the baby on to her feet.

'What colour would you say she was?' David asked Polly, stepping over the twins who by now were kneeling in the straw.

Polly helped Lady Jane to clean the baby, rubbing her sides with handfuls of straw, drying the wet body until the fluffy fur showed dark grey. 'Blue roan,' she said. 'With a white star on her forehead and four white socks; see!'

The twins nodded eagerly. Each of the foal's gangling, stick-like grey legs ended in a clean white sock.

'Look at her sweet little stubbly mane!' Hannah breathed, edging further forward.

'Stay back. She's getting up again!' Helen warned. This time, the foal folded her legs under body then

pushed until they were straight. She wobbled, tottered and fell.

'Ahh!' Helen and Hannah sighed.

Polly grinned and looked up at her mum.

'Again!' Linda Moone encouraged, nodding at Lady Jane. The mare used her long nose to nudge her baby into another attempt to stand. 'Third time lucky!'

The foal struggled to her feet. She swayed, she staggered, her legs buckled then straightened. She stood full square.

'Made it!' Polly's smile broadened.

'Fantastic!' David zoomed in on the moment of triumph.

'Unbelievable!' Hannah murmured with tears in her eyes.

Helen wanted to rush in and hug the brave little foal. 'What a star!'

'That would be a good name for her, actually,' Mrs Moone said, picking up on Helen's remark. She looked fondly at the still-groggy grey foal as it tottered and stretched out its head towards its mother. 'With that white marking on her forehead, and given that she was born two weeks early, I think we should get William Baxter to call her Star the Surprise!'

Five

'Mum, can we have a lift into the village?' Hannah asked early next morning.

Mary Moore was about to set off for work. She grabbed her car keys from the kitchen table and took a last mouthful of toast. 'What for? Are you going to try and make up with Laura?'

'No, we're off to see Star!' Helen brought in a gust of fresh air as she stepped in from the yard. 'Fed the hens, fed the geese, fed the rabbits, fed Sunny, fed Solo!' She reeled off the list of chores she'd already got through.

Their mum stopped in the doorway and looked hard at her rosy, excited face. 'Star's this new foal at Manor Farm, right?'

'Yes, and she's gorgeous!' Hannah jumped up and grabbed her red fleece jacket. 'She's soft and fluffy and grey—'

'Blue roan!' Helen corrected.

'. . . With a white star and white socks and the cutest little face you've ever seen!'

'And what about Polly?' Mary narrowed her eyes and reminded them of the one bugbear.

Hannah hesitated then zipped up her jacket. 'Oh, she's not bad really.'

'No?' Mary's eyebrows shot up. 'Helen?'

Helen dumped the empty water bucket on to the stone-flagged floor. 'Yeah, Polly's OK when you get to know her.'

'Well, stone the crows!' their mum exclaimed. She winked at their dad as he came downstairs in his socks, hair tousled, a speck of shaving foam still on his chin. 'Would you believe it? The twins have changed their minds about Polly Moone!'

'Hi, Mrs Moone. Where's Polly?' Helen asked brightly, standing on the doorstep at Manor Farm.

A sudden, sharp April shower had begun as the twins' mum dropped them off by the double gates of

Doveton Manor. They were already soaked to the skin as they took the short cut to the farm along the bridleway by the side of the Saunderses' house. They hadn't stopped to seek Laura out and say hi, although they could see Sultan's stable door open and hear sounds from inside. Instead, they'd hurried on along the lakeside to the Moones' place.

Linda Moone smiled down at the two dripping girls from the shelter of her wide, dry hallway. Rain had flattened their short dark hair and trickled down their foreheads and off the ends of their noses. Still their brown eyes looked eager as they hopped up and down on the step. 'Polly's out in the stableyard,' she told them. 'I'm surprised you didn't see her.'

'OK, thanks!' Hannah tugged Helen sideways and towed her off towards the stables.

'Mind the . . . huge puddle!' Mrs Moone warned.

Too late. The twins rounded the corner of the converted barn which housed the new swimming-pool and landed ankle deep in the biggest puddle around. It stretched from the corner of the pool conversion ten metres across the concrete yard to an overflowing drain in the middle.

'Drainage problem.' A tall man stood, arms folded, watching Helen and Hannah paddle clear. He was wearing a green waxed jacket, wellingtons and a checked cap, pulled well down over a thin bony face. 'I've just been on the phone to the builder. He's on his way over to take a look.'

'Whoops!' Hannah's trainers squelched as she stepped back on to dry land.

'We're looking for Polly,' Helen explained nervously. The man's deep voice and sharp-eyed glance made her uneasy.

'Ah, after my daughter? Well, she's in the end stable.' Mr Moone nodded in the right direction, then decided to lead the way. Obviously put out by the flood, he grumbled about second-rate builders laying sub-standard drainage pipes. 'Weekend, or no weekend, I want that builder to come and sort it out straight away.'

Helen and Hannah squelched after him without comment, glad when they finally spotted Polly in Lady Jane's stable. She had heard their wet footsteps and was peering over the door.

'Hi, you two!' She greeted them with a little grin, but without surprise. 'You couldn't keep away, huh?'

'Hi, Polly. How's Star?' Hannah ran the last few steps to the door.

'She's . . . fine.' Standing to one side, Polly let the

twins see the mare and foal standing quietly together.

'You don't sound sure.' Helen had picked up a tiny hesitation.

'Well, she *is* fine. . . honestly!'

'*But*?' Hannah frowned. Little Star stood shakily, looking a bit lost inside the spacious stable, despite her mother's efforts to protect her from the newcomers' gaze.

'But Lady Jane isn't,' Polly confessed.

'Why? What's wrong with her?' Helen switched her attention to the mare.

'We're not sure. She seems to be running a temperature and she's not very interested in letting Star feed.' Polly opened the door to allow Helen and Hannah in. 'Whenever the foal tries to suckle, Lady Jane moves away.'

'So what'll happen?' Helen asked, feeling her good mood evaporate. A foal needed plenty of chance to feed in the first days of life; she knew that much.

'Mum's not that worried yet, but she called the vet to make sure. Sally Freeman's on her way right now.' Polly passed on the news without any sign of panic. 'Don't worry,' she told Hannah and Helen. 'If it turns out that Lady Jane does have a problem feeding Star herself, we can bottle-rear her.'

'Oh. Right.' Hannah felt that this was a lot to take in. She'd come expecting to find the sweet little foal enjoying her first view of the world; maybe poking her nose out into the fresh air, taking a hop and a skip across the yard. Instead, this talk of feeding problems and fever made Hannah's heart miss a couple of beats.

Lost in thought, she scarcely heard a car arrive at the house.

'Maybe that's Sally!' Helen ran off to look and soon came back with a disappointed shake of her head. 'Sally drives a Land Rover. This is a white van.'

'Ah!' Mr Moone, who had stood to one side listening to Polly's news, spoke up. 'That must be Cookson, the builder!' He turned and strode away.

Meanwhile, Polly took the twins next door to a storeroom stacked at one end with bales of hay and at the other with plastic sacks of wood shavings. 'We may as well change Lady Jane's bedding while we're waiting for the vet,' she suggested.

'How come you're taking this so calmly?' Hannah wanted to know. She helped Polly shift and break open a bag of shavings.

'Because I've seen this sort of thing before,' Polly explained. 'When we lived in the city I used to help out at weekends at a livery stables on the outskirts. I've bottle-fed a couple of foals when the mothers weren't well, so I know what to do.'

'But what about Lady Jane?'

'Hmm.' Polly nodded. 'That's more of a worry, I agree. We just have to hope it isn't anything serious.'

'Well, we won't have long to wait before we find out. Sally's here now.' Helen looked out to see the vet's Land Rover drive into the yard and splash straight through the deep puddle, past Mr Moone and the builder.

Hannah and Polly broke off from forking wood shavings into a wheelbarrow and came out of the storeroom in time to see Linda Moone introduce herself to the Doveton vet.

'I hope I'm not making a fuss over nothing,' she said, leading the way to Lady Jane's stable. 'Only, I did think I was better to be on the safe side, since the mare doesn't actually belong to us. In fact, her owner would never forgive us if anything were to go wrong.'

'That's quite all right.' Sally Freeman smiled at the twins, then took off her jacket and set to work. 'This horse is certainly losing condition,' she agreed, checking the inside of Lady Jane's eyelids and examining her dull coat. Quickly she took her temperature and confirmed that it was way above normal. 'Her udder's tight and the teats look sore. No wonder she doesn't want the foal to feed.'

'So what's causing it?' Quietly Linda listened to the list of symptoms, crouching and keeping one arm around Star's neck to restrain her.

Sally stood back from Lady Jane and shook her head. 'It could be any number of things. Complications inside the uterus, for example. That could set up an infection which would cause the high temperature. But our immediate problem is to make sure that the foal gets the all-important first feed, which I don't think she has done yet.' She too crouched and pointed to the mare's udder.

'Can't we just bottle-feed Star and leave Lady Jane to get better?' Polly asked.

'No, because the first milk from the mother contains important antibodies which protect the foal from disease.' Moving smoothly and skilfully, Sally managed to extract the thick milk from the udder. Though she was small and slight, she showed no fear as she dealt with the strong thoroughbred.

Standing back, Helen wrinkled her nose. Hannah watched through half-closed eyes. Only when the liquid was safely inside a sterile bottle and a rubber teat fixed on, did they relax and dare to watch properly.

'OK, Polly; I can see you're raring to go. You get to give Star her first bottle.' Sally asked her to take over while she turned her attention to the sick horse.

With fingers crossed, Helen and Hannah watched Polly take charge. Holding tight to the full bottle, she took her mother's place at the foal's side, hooking one arm around Star's neck and tilting the teat against her lips.

At first the foal shook her head and struggled, but Polly held tight. Then a drop of milk leaked through

the teat on to the tip of Star's pink tongue. An alert look came over her, her furry ears pricked up, as she fixed her eyes firmly on Polly, her tongue slowly licking her lips. Polly held the bottle steady, easing the teat ever so carefully between Star's lips until she suddenly snatched at it and started to suck.

'Ho-oh!' Hannah and Helen breathed loud sighs of relief.

Down, down, down went the level of white liquid in the bottle.

'Good work!' Sally Freeman told Polly. She stood back from Lady Jane and consulted with Linda Moone.

Hannah and Helen were so thrilled with the way Star had taken the bottle that they hardly heard the grown-ups' muttered conversation.

'Bacterial infection of the uterus . . . Nothing you did wrong . . . it happens sometimes.' The vet's voice was easier to pick up, while Mrs Moone's stayed low and anxious. She mentioned the name of William Baxter, Lady Jane's owner, and said that since he was out of the country he would be difficult to contact.

'The foal will need special care, of course.' Sally broke away from Linda Moone to see how Polly was getting on. 'She'll have to be bottle-fed while we perform a straightforward piece of minor surgery on her mother. Then we put the mare on a course of strong antibiotics to cure the infection. In fact, it's most likely that the foal will have to be hand-reared until she's ready to be weaned in a few months' time. Do you think you can manage that?'

Straightaway Polly nodded, then released Star from her firm hold as she held up the empty bottle.

The foal tottered sideways towards Hannah and Helen, overbalancing in the soft bed of shavings at their feet. They both dropped to the ground to help her up and brush her down.

'It looks like you have some willing volunteers to assist you at any rate!' Sally Freeman laughed.

Polly grinned at Helen picking curls of wood shavings out of Star's spiky grey mane and Hannah dusting off the foal's stumpy tail. 'How about it?' she asked. 'Can you spare some time from your pony and your dog and your cat and all the other Home Farm animals you're always rabbiting on about to come and help feed Star?'

Helen turned to Hannah. *Us?* she was about to protest. *Go on and on about Solo and Speckle? Never! Anyway, what about you and your precious Holly?*

But Hannah gave her a much-practised, sharp dig with her elbow.

'Ouch!' Helen yelped instead.

Hannah stepped in with a rapid answer to Polly's question. 'Sure we can spare the time!' she assured her. 'In fact, Polly, we'd love to help you hand-rear Star!'

Six

'"We'd *lurve* to help you hand-rear Star!"' Helen teased. '"We'd really, really *lu-urve* to!"'

'Don't care!' Hannah said, head in the air.

'Did you have to . . . gush?' Helen sought for and found the perfect word.

'La-la; don't care!' Hannah sang. No matter what Helen said, she was happy. There was a fantastic spring ahead of them, and all because Polly had asked them to help her bottle-feed Star.

It was a breezy Sunday morning. They were riding Solo down by the lake, too intent on reaching Manor Farm to notice Laura riding Sultan in the opposite direction until it was too late to call after her and yell hello.

'Oops!' Helen muttered when she realised how it must look.

'It's not funny,' Hannah insisted. For a second she considered turning Solo around and cantering up the fell after Laura. But then she suspected she wouldn't get a very warm welcome if she did.

'No, I know it's not.' Helen sighed and went on pushing the bike over the pebbles. Manor Farm was in sight, and although it was only half past nine, the yard was already a hive of activity.

A riding class was about to start, to judge by the number of horses and riders of all sizes gathered there; from Welsh cobs to Shetlands, from middle-aged men to pint-sized six-year-olds.

And there, in the midst of it all, was Polly; organising and checking, giving leg-ups, re-fastening throatlashes, lengthening stirrups.

'Hi, you two!' she called out to Hannah and Helen. 'Hey, great; you brought Solo. He'd love to join the ride, wouldn't you, boy?'

And before Hannah had time to think, Polly was checking the pony's girth and leading him into line, ready to hack out.

'W-w-what about Star?' Hannah mumbled. Solo was

wedged between a giant bay cob and a spritely Connemara pony ridden by Kylie Leech, the twins' classmate at Doveton Junior.

'*I* can feed Star!' Helen volunteered like a flash. She was halfway across the yard, sprinting for the stable.

Leaving her mother to make final arrangements for the ride, Polly followed Helen. As they went into Lady Jane and Star's stall, they slowed down and spoke just above a whisper.

'How is she?' Helen asked, turning first to the dejected-looking mare.

'OK. As well as can be expected.' Polly went to stroke the grey horse's neck. 'Sally came back with the equipment she needed to do the surgery late last night. She popped in again this morning and said that everything is going well. The antibiotics should begin to work later today.'

Helen nodded. 'That's good. And how's Star?'

'Brilliant!' Polly's face took on a broad smile as Helen went to rub the foal's soft nose. 'She takes her feed like a dream. I'll show you where we keep the bottles and stuff so you can feed her while we're out.'

Nodding again, Helen told herself that she would manage the job by herself. She'd pictured the three of them doing it together; herself, Hannah and Polly.

But no, she could do it alone. Carefully she listened to Polly's instructions, then went to see Hannah off on the ride.

'Solo looks great!' Polly told them, having fetched Holly out of her stable and ridden up alongside. 'He's really fit and well turned out.'

'Thanks.' Hannah had made a special effort with his grooming that morning.

'He looks like he'll do well in the jumping competition at the gymkhana next month.'

'What gymkhana?' Helen took hold of Solo's reins to stop him backing into Kylie and her light brown pony, Hobnob.

'Nesfield Gymkhana. Kylie was telling me all about it. They have a great pony-class competition, don't they, Kylie?'

The red-haired girl nodded. 'I've entered Hobnob.'

'You mean to say you haven't entered Solo!' Polly exclaimed.

'Well . . . er . . . no!' It hadn't crossed Helen's or Hannah's mind. Gymkhanas were for *real* horsey people, not for them. You needed transport for a start; a horse-box and all the proper stuff.

'But he looks like he's got Irish blood, and Connemaras are excellent jumpers,' Polly claimed as the ride moved off. 'I bet he'd do really well!'

Helen let go of Solo's reins and watched Hannah walk him on. Their pony *did* look smart; every bit as good as Hobnob, for instance. And he was strong and fit. And he could jump. She and Hannah had tried him over ditches and low stone walls on the fellside. *Hmm*. She turned away, head down, thoughtful. It was time to feed Star. But Solo in the pony class at Nesfield . . . *Hmm*. The seed was sown.

For the last two weeks of April, through into May, Hannah and Helen spent every spare minute with Polly Moone at Manor Farm.

'Look, if the horse-box is a problem, why not share ours?' Polly had suggested when they'd told her that they couldn't possibly enter Solo in the competition. 'We've got loads of space in our box. You can ride Solo down from Home Farm and load him up here for the journey to Nesfield!'

David and Mary Moore had hesitated over the offer. 'It's not good to be too much in someone's debt,' Mary had pointed out. 'It makes things lop-sided.'

'But Polly says we're helping her when we go down to feed Star!' Helen had argued. 'She says that they're the ones who owe us something in return!'

'But how could you train Solo to showjump in three or four weeks?' David had pinpointed the other major difficulty.

'No problem!' Hannah had insisted. 'Polly says she'll teach us!'

And it had been settled. Solo was to jump in the gymkhana and Polly was to train them. That meant spending every spare minute at Manor Farm, riding Solo over jumps set up in the field that the Moones rented from the Saunders.

'Great!' Mary said one Saturday evening, as she stopped by on her way home from work to watch. She'd seen Solo soar over a water jump and leap a

triple pole. She waited for Helen to dismount and took both girls to one side as Polly raised the jumps ready to ride Holly round. 'But who's going to do the actual riding on the day itself?'

A breathless Helen took off her hard hat and glanced quickly at Hannah. They'd been backing off from the decision for ages. 'We haven't decided yet.'

Their mum put her head to one side. 'Could be a *bi-ig problemo*!'

But in the event, it wasn't.

'Hannah, *you* should ride Solo!' Polly declared. She'd overheard Mary Moore posing the thorny question and jumped in with her opinion. 'You've spent more time practising. Helen's been too busy looking after Star!'

'True.' Reluctantly Helen admitted that every time they came down to Manor Farm, her first thought was for the foal. She was usually the one who left Polly and Hannah discussing tactics for the competition and went to make up the bottle. Her mind was always fixed on going into the stable and coaxing little Star to take her full feed. Each time she slipped the teat into the foal's mouth and felt the tug on the bottle, she felt a kind of magical calm.

'Yep,' she agreed. 'Hannah, you do it. But just make sure you win!'

'Wake up, it's the big day!' David Moore announced as he strode across the twins' bedroom and flung open the curtains. 'Nesfield Gymkhana. Come on, rise and shine!'

'Du-dah!' Hannah and Helen sprang out from behind the door, already fully dressed. Hannah was wearing black jodphurs and a fawn polo shirt, Helen was in her everyday jeans and a yellow T-shirt.

'We didn't sleep a wink,' Hannah told him.

'Hannah didn't,' Helen grumbled. 'I would have if she hadn't kept on tossing and turning all night.'

Their dad nodded 'It's no wonder you're nervous, Hann. First time ever that you've entered a jumping competition, and everyone you know will be there watching.'

'Thanks, Dad!' She was already wishing that she hadn't let Polly Moone browbeat her into this.

'You'll be fine!' Mary popped her head round the door. 'You've worked really hard to get Solo ready, and Polly's been a good teacher, hasn't she?'

Taking a deep breath, Hannah nodded. Hours and hours of jumping practice in the bottom field at Manor

Farm should pay off. These days she practically ate and slept cavalletti jumps, then, as she'd made progress, walls and brushes, rails and parallel bars.

'Good, so I plan to take time out from the cafe to come and watch you,' her mum promised, rushing off to work as usual. 'Oh, by the way, I almost forgot; Polly rang to ask if you two would mind leaving the gymkhana early.'

'How come?' Helen asked.

'Something to do with her mum having entered the adult competition, which takes place in the afternoon. You'll be finished by lunchtime, apparently. So she wonders if you'd mind coming back to Doveton to give Star her midday feed.'

'Fine.' Helen and Hannah nodded.

'I told her it would probably be OK for Dad to drive you back.' Mary came and gave Hannah a hug. 'So, good luck and do your best.'

'I will,' Hannah promised. But she needed to take several more deep breaths before she could stop her hands from shaking and make her voice sound normal.

'Breakfast!' Her dad ordered her downstairs. 'And no saying you're not hungry!'

* * *

The morning raced by. Hannah hardly noticed her breakfast of boiled egg and toast, or the journey by car down to Manor Farm. It was Helen who had checked Solo's tack and ridden him down the lane, arriving just before Hannah and her father. And it was Helen who had helped load Solo into the horse-box alongside Holly, bandaging his legs and tail for the half-hour journey over the fells to Nesfield. The horses sensed the excitement of the day and went in willingly, each looking the picture of health and good grooming.

'All set?' Linda Moone asked, climbing into the driver's seat and ordering Polly into the passenger seat beside her.

Helen nodded.

'Nervous' Mr Moone asked Hannah, as for the umpteenth time she checked that she had her hard hat and crop on the back seat of her dad's car. There they were, beside his camera and bag of equipment.

Hannah gulped and nodded.

'Well, good luck!' Richard Moone wished her well. 'I'll miss the start of the pony competition, I'm afraid. I have to wait here for Cookson to show up.'

'Problems?' David Moore held the car door open for Helen and Hannah.

The tall, skinny man shrugged. 'Builders, you know. He still hasn't sorted out this trouble with the drains. But nevertheless, I should reach Nesfield in time for Hannah's final rounds.'

'If I get that far!' Hannah muttered to Helen as she hunched in the back seat.

'What do you mean, "If"? Course you will!' Helen insisted. Slowly the horse-box crept out of the stable-yard, down the drive towards the road. Their dad followed, driving steadily past the wide gates of Doveton Manor under a bright and breezy sky. 'You and Solo are going to win first prize, remember!'

Seven

Nesfield Gymkhana took place in May each year on a field by the shore of Lake Rydal. It drew competitors from all over the Lake District and, because of its pretty setting, people came to watch from even further afield.

'Busy, busy!' David Moore tapped the steering-wheel as he followed Linda Moone's horse-box through the narrow town streets. Inside the box, the twins could glimpse the swaying rumps of Holly and Solo as the vehicle tackled a bend and then a tight corner.

'Hey, isn't that the Saunderses' box behind us?' Helen twisted round in her seat and pointed to a smart maroon truck, and to Laura's father, Geoffrey, at the wheel.

Hannah sank down out of sight. 'Thank goodness Solo and I aren't in the same competition as Laura!'

'How come you're not?' David drove down a lane and through a gate into a rough field next to the jumping arena.

'Sultan's in the thoroughbred class, along with Polly,' Helen explained.

'Is that so? We'll expect to see some fireworks when Polly and Laura come face to face, then, shall we?'

Luckily, there was too much to do for Helen and Hannah to consider this. Solo and Holly had to be unloaded and watered for a start. The twins watched Polly and Linda Moone lower the ramp of the horse-box, then leaped out of the car to help.

As they worked, they overheard their dad greet Geoffrey Saunders, who had pulled up his truck nearby.

'David? Hello! I didn't expect to see you here today. Laura didn't mention it.' Mr Saunders took a look around the busy car park, leaving his daughter to tend to Sultan. 'Come to think about it, I haven't seen hide nor hair of the twins at the Manor lately . . .'

Helen blushed and tried to block her ears. But as

she led Solo down the ramp, ears pricked and head up, who should they bump into but Laura herself. 'Hi,' Helen mumbled, her face burning now.

Laura gave Helen a long, blank stare.

'Sorry!' In her rush to squeeze past, Helen let Solo barge into Sultan, who pulled at his leadrope and reared up.

'Hey, watch out!' a voice cried from further down the line of recently-arrived horses.

Laura scowled, brought Sultan under control, then turned to apologise in a loud voice. 'Oh, Gwyneth, it's you. Look, I'm sorry about that. You know how it is when people can't keep their ponies under control!'

Helen caught Hannah's eye and glowered. She remembered the name, Gwyneth Turner, from Polly's ramblings at school. If she'd got it right, Gwyneth and her grey horse, Minty, had won last year's under-thirteen competition. 'Here; you take Solo!' she hissed at Hannah. 'I'll fetch his saddle.'

In the end, Hannah did manage to lead Solo out of harm's way, but not before she'd been treated to the worst display of showing off she'd heard for a long time.

'. . . Oh, sure!' The girl with smooth blonde hair and a smart black jacket had laughed mockingly.

'Some people shouldn't be allowed to enter gymkhanas at all, if you ask me!' She'd had her uneasy grey eyes fixed on Hannah and Solo all the time she'd talked. She seemed nervous, but determined not to let it show.

'I know. Beginners!' Laura had joined in nastily, carefully keeping her back to Hannah and Helen.

'Wasting their time!' Gwyneth had been relieved to find an ally in Laura. 'And getting in other people's way!' She'd deliberately kept her horse standing in Solo's path, allowing the grey thoroughbred to reach out and meanly nip the pony's face.

'Let me go home right now!' Hannah moaned at Helen when at last she'd got Solo in the paddock for competitors. Laura and Gwyneth were still huddled together by the horse-boxes.

'Did you hear what they said about Polly?' Helen gasped, pushing through the crowd with Solo's heavy saddle. 'They said she and Holly didn't stand a chance in the thoroughbred section later this morning.'

'Sour grapes, that's all,' Hannah replied. 'Really, I'll bet they're scared stiff of losing.'

'Who's scared stiff of losing?' Another voice chimed in, and Kylie Leech from school pushed through the crowd with a wide grin on her face. 'You?'

'No!' Helen shot back, jutting out her chin as she eyed Kylie's black velvet hard hat and tailored jacket. 'Are we, Hann?'

Taking her numbered vest from the steward, who then ticked off her name, Hannah waited quietly for Helen to fasten Solo's girth and, with trembling legs, she swung up into the saddle. 'No way!' she vowed.

But she felt her stomach churn and her palms grow clammy as the announcer cleared his throat and asked the first competitor in the pony class to come to the start.

The next hour thundered by in a rush of hooves and creaking saddles. Bells sounded, the crowd fell quiet, ponies went into the ring and jumped. Walls fell, fences thudded to the ground.

'Four faults!' the steward reported. Or, 'Twelve faults for Jonathan King on Punch. . . ! A time fault for Maggie Warner on Katie!'

'Go, Hannah, go!' Helen urged her into the ring. There were three clear rounds so far, with only Solo and another pony left to jump.

Hannah and Solo took off. They soared over two brush fences and a wall, hesitated at parallel bars, then took them in their stride. Solo came to the edge

of the arena, turned and sprinted back towards the water-jump. He cleared it with plenty to spare. In the saddle, Hannah flexed her knees and thrust her weight forward, felt him leap, sat back as he landed. A perfect jump. And she was making good time. More of the same still to do; another high wall which Solo just tipped with his front hooves, before he galloped on at breakneck speed.

'And a clear round for Hannah Moore on Solo!' the steward called as they made their final clearance. 'So we'll see them again in the jump-off!'

'Brilliant!' Helen crowed. She just hoped Laura and the dreadful Gwyneth Turner had been around to see it.

'Well done, love!' Mary Moore had slipped away from the Curlew in time to catch Hannah's magnificent round.

'Great. I got some terrific shots!' David held up his camera.

'Only the jump-off to go now!' Helen urged. 'How do you feel, Hann?'

Hannah slid from the saddle and patted Solo's hot neck. 'My legs are like jelly and I'm shaking like a leaf!' she confessed. 'Otherwise, I feel just fine!'

* * *

Solo was last to go in the jump-off. He and Hannah needed a fast time and under six faults to win a prize. Kylie Leech and Hobnob had just done a good round which had put them into second place.

'Go, Hannah! Go, Solo!' Helen cried at the sound of the final bell.

The jumps were higher than before. They looked like prison walls towering overhead, until the moment when Solo took off, clipping them with his heels and landing safely each time. Hannah rode him hard, skimming the brushwood, swerving round corners, charging at the water-jump.

Splash! Solo's back feet landed in the ditch.

'Aah!' the crowd cried in disappointment for the brave little pony.

Hannah rode on. They could still get third or even second place.

'. . . Four faults gives first-time entrants Hannah and Solo second prize in the Under-Thirteen Pony Competition!' the steward cried, to loud cheers from the crowd.

'Second!' David Moore rushed forward to take photographs.

Click-click! He got pictures of Helen running to

hug Hannah, then Solo. Mary stood, hands clasped and smiling.

'Wow!' Helen yelled. 'You did it, Hann! Solo, you proved them all wrong!'

They were still in a daze, even after the judge had pinned a blue rosette on to Solo's bridle, and had only just come back down to earth when the next competition started.

'Well done, Hannah!' Polly beamed down at her from Holly's back as she queued for her turn in the thoroughbred contest. 'Second prize is fantastic, considering it's your first outing!'

'Thanks to you!' Hannah grinned back, ignoring the scowls from both Laura and Gwyneth Turner, whose horses bunched impatiently behind Polly and Holly.

Helen and Hannah just had time to wish Polly luck before Laura and Gwyneth pushed by. Then they stayed to watch the first thoroughbred begin the tough course. It was, as it turned out, Gwyneth Turner's horse Minty. The eager grey clipped the early fences, then came a real cropper at a high wall. He mistimed it and cannoned into the imitation bricks, bringing the whole thing down. After that, he lost his nerve and finished the round with eighteen faults.

Hannah made a face at Helen but said nothing. It was Laura's turn next and, in spite of everything, they hoped that Sultan would fare better than poor Minty.

Yet they could tell from the start that Laura wasn't relaxed. She held Sultan's reins too tight and couldn't get a good rhythm as she approached the first jump. Sultan cleared it but landed awkwardly. Then he wasn't in his proper stride for the second fence. At the last minute he turned his head. Laura gave him a kick. He plunged on, straight into the striped poles, bringing them crashing down.

'Uh-oh.' Hannah could hardly bear to look as Sultan and Laura clocked up more faults at the water-jump. They finished with sixteen faults against them.

'Hannah-Helen!' David Moore rushed up before they had time to comment. Laura was just sweeping by on Sultan, head down, staring at the ground. 'Have you seen the time? It's nearly twelve. You should be over at Manor Farm feeding Star by now!'

They were glad to go, leaving Mrs Moone to keep an eye on Solo, then weaving through the crowd after their dad. 'Good luck, Polly! We'll be back later!' they called, then dived into the car for the journey to Doveton. Exhausted after the excitement of the gymkhana, they didn't say much until David dropped them off by Manor Farm.

'I'm popping home for more film for my camera,' he told them. 'See you back here in twenty minutes.'

That was just time to make up the feed in a clear plastic bottle, give it to the hungry foal, then walk Lady Jane down to the bottom field to spend the afternoon grazing there, as Mrs Moone had requested. They walked quickly across the yard, happy to see the grey mare poke her head over the stable door and snicker a greeting.

'I'll do the bottle!' Helen volunteered, while Hannah raked out the soiled wood shavings and forked a fresh layer on to the bed. Little Star hopped and skipped out of the way of the rake, her skinny legs shooting her off the ground, head to one side, her huge, dark eyes gleaming.

Then, when Helen brought the bottle into the stable, she ran to her, nudging and pushing until she seized the teat and began to suck. Meanwhile, Lady Jane stood watching, as if quietly supervising her foal's meal-time.

'Good girl!' Helen said gently.

Glug-glug-glug; the milk disappeared from the bottle.

'All gone!' she cooed.

Star licked her lips, then, seeing that lunch was over, skipped over to the corner for an energetic roll in the new bed. She stood up again, covered in cream-coloured shavings, sneezing and swishing her short tail.

Hannah smiled. Reaching for Lady Jane's headcollar, she fastened it on. 'Come down to the field and open the gate for us,' she told Helen. 'Come on, quickly. Dad'll be back any minute.'

Sensing an afternoon in the sun, the mare came willingly, walking gracefully across the concrete yard as Hannah led her and Helen stayed to bolt Star inside the warm, safe stable.

'Be good!' Helen warned the playful foal, who trotted up to the door and grabbed her sleeve. 'Your mum deserves a peaceful afternoon off while you stay here.' Pulling free, she ran after Hannah and Lady Jane, darting ahead in time to open the gate to the bottom, rented field where the mare was to enjoy her peace and quiet.

They waited there only long enough to make sure that the horse was happy in the field before they hurried back to the stableyard.

'I think I just heard a car,' Hannah gasped, out

of breath from running.

'It must be Dad.' Helen couldn't see over the wall, but she put on more speed. '. . . Nope!' When she got to the yard, there was no car to be seen. 'Nothing!'

'I'm sure I heard someone . . .' Hannah overtook Helen and stood in the middle of the empty yard. She put her hands on her hips to try to catch her breath, then looked all around. 'Hey, Helen, did you fasten Star's stable door?'

'Yep.' Helen remembered clearly the sound of the bolt sliding shut.

'Well, that's funny . . .' Slowly Hannah went across. 'It's open now!'

'It can't be!' Helen felt a stab of alarm. For a second she didn't move. Then she jerked forward after Hannah.

'Yes, wide open.' Hannah stared at the door swinging in the breeze. She turned to Helen. 'What's going on?'

'Nothing. Don't worry. I'm sure everything's . . . OK!' Helen's breathless protests came to a sudden stop. She was the first to reach Star's stable, the first to look inside and gasp in surprise.

'It's empty!' Hannah came up behind her and groaned the words. She looked in every corner;

looked twice and then a third time. 'Helen, what's happened to Star?'

'Gone!' The short, whispered reply made it horribly true, though Helen could still hardly believe her eyes.

'How? Where?' Hannah couldn't catch her breath to say more.

Helplessly Helen shook her head.

They stood quite still, shocked and not knowing where to turn, aware only that the tiny thoroughbred foal had just vanished into thin air.

Eight

'They trusted us to look after Star!' Hannah's first thought was that they had let Polly, Linda and Richard Moone down.

'I'm sure I closed the door!' Helen shut it now and slid the bolt across. She was still so shocked she could hardly think.

Hannah frowned. 'Say you made a mistake,' she suggested quietly. 'Maybe you thought you'd fastened it, but really the bolt missed the slot. Then Star could've pushed the door open again while we were down at the field, and run away!'

'Oh no!' Shaken by the foal's sudden disappearance, Helen could only gasp. Her mind whirled over the possibilities; little Star trotting out across the yard to look for her mother, choosing the wrong direction, heading for the road . . . !

At the instant she thought of the dangers of traffic on the main road, she heard a car driving into the yard.

'Dad!' Hannah ran for help. 'Star's gone!'

'What do you mean, "gone"?' Their father got out of the car with a puzzled look.

'Vanished . . . run away, maybe! Did you see any sign of her out on the main road?' *Please, please say yes*! She clenched her hands and held her breath.

'No, not a thing.' Slowly David took in what had happened. He leaned into the empty stable to check.

'Are you sure?' Hannah ran to each corner of the yard, looking in storerooms, startling the horses in the other stables. 'Star can't have vanished into thin air!'

'I'm absolutely certain I closed the door!' Helen repeated time after time. 'Unless I'm going mad!'

'But that would mean someone coming along and deliberately opening it while we were away!' Hannah pointed out. She'd stopped racing round the yard and come back to where Helen still stood in shock.

'Which would also mean that this someone was up

to no good,' David Moore added, taking up Hannah's train of thought.

Hannah nodded. 'They must have checked that the coast was clear, then moved in. And Dad, we did hear a car! We thought it was you, but when we got here, it had already gone!'

'Hmm.' His frown deepened and he bit his bottom lip. 'A car, or something bigger?'

'Bigger!' Hannah remembered the low, chugging sound of the engine.

'Big enough to be a horse-box or a Land Rover pulling a trailer?' David asked.

As Hannah nodded, Helen broke in. 'What are you saying?'

'Nothing, yet. We're trying to work it out.' Her dad went into Star's stable to examine the bolt from the inside and convince himself that it hadn't been forced open.

'Yes, you are!' Helen turned round on the spot. She took in the smart white stable doors, the converted barn, the fells rising in the distance Overhead the white clouds raced dizzily across a blue sky. 'You're saying you think Star's been stolen!'

'Now, let's not be hasty,' David pleaded as the twins

piled into the car and they drove fast towards Nesfield. He, Hannah and Helen had all searched in every last corner for the lost foal and were now dreading having to pass on the bad news to the Moones. Yet they knew they must do it as soon as possible.

Helen hung on as the car took a hairpin bend in the road over Rydal Fell. They threaded their way through rugged Hardstone Pass, then swooped into the green valley below. 'Star needs her next bottle in four hours!' she reminded them. 'What'll happen if she doesn't get fed?'

Neither her dad nor Hannah replied.

'Who would do this?' Hannah's mind was racing off along another track. 'Who would steal a helpless little foal?'

'Like I said, let's not jump to conclusions.' David concentrated on more sharp bends. The town of Nesfield came into view, its cluster of stone houses clinging to the shore of Lake Rydal. 'The important thing is to pass on the exact facts as we know them.'

But Hannah wasn't listening. 'It could be a proper horse thief,' she suggested, swaying against Helen as the car tilted. 'But a professional wouldn't have stolen Star; she's too young and still needs looking after. They would have taken Lady Jane or one of the other fully-grown thoroughbreds.'

Grimly Helen nodded. 'So it's probably someone who knows Polly and wants to get back at her.'

'Like Gwyneth Turner,' Hannah said more slowly, thinking of all the people Polly had upset. She recalled the blonde girl's spiteful remarks as the twins and Polly had unloaded their horses. 'Until the Moones arrived, she was the star jumper around here. She could easily have a grudge against Polly after what happened to her and Minty in the competition this morning.'

'Girls!' their dad protested, slowing down for the town traffic. 'That's complete rubbish! It's money that a thief would be after, so forget all this nonsense about Gwyneth Turner!'

For a few moments, Hannah and Helen fell quiet. But the silence only let their minds race on. Here was the entrance to the gymkhana and the crowded car park. Here was their parking space on the rough grass plot, and there was an empty gap and tyre marks where the Saunderses' maroon horse-box had stood.

'They must have gone home early,' Hannah said, sensing that Helen had spotted the truck's absence at the same split second. 'There was nothing for them to hang around for after Sultan made a mess of his round.'

'Right!' Helen breathed. She sat in the car, staring out, hearing the faint voice of the steward over the loudspeakers. 'So they could have got back to Doveton Manor around the same time as us!'

'Hannah, Helen, I've already warned you not to let your imaginations run riot!' their dad warned. 'I know you're worried about Star, but please try to be sensible!'

'Maybe that was the Saunderses' truck we heard in the lane,' Hannah whispered, so anxious that she hardly heard a word of her dad's advice. In her mind's eye she pictured a figure slipping along the bridleway and spying on her and Helen as they led Lady Jane down to the bottom field. The figure saw her chance to creep into the Moones' stableyard, right up to Star's door. Headcollar in hand, she slid back the bolt and stepped inside. Seconds later she was leading the tiny blue roan foal out, spiriting her away before the twins returned.

Helen sat tight beside Hannah as their dad wove slowly through the crowd towards the arena. They turned to each other and stared.

'Laura!' they gasped as the dreadful possibility hit home. 'Oh, she wouldn't . . . would she?'

* * *

'Dad, wait!' Helen and Hannah ran after him through the throng of spectators. They could see Richard Moone standing beside his wife, both intently watching the activity in the arena. The bell had just rung for the next competitor to enter.

'Dad, you can tell Mr and Mrs Moone, but let us tell Polly!' Hannah caught him up just in time.

'Are you sure?' He turned and paused.

Helen nodded. 'This is all our fault, so we should be the ones!'

David shrugged. 'Well, in any case, I planned to wait a few minutes.' Pointing out that Holly was the next horse to trot into the arena, he took out his camera and prepared to take pictures. 'It looks like the final jump-off.'

'Polly needs a clear round in under sixty-five seconds to win the competition!' The excited voice of the steward announced the tense situation. 'It's a tall order for this young rider and her chestnut mare!'

'She'll never do it!' a voice in the crowd muttered.

'But she'll have a go!' someone else said, as a second bell rang and the clock began to tick. 'She's a plucky little thing, though you'd never think it to look at her.'

Polly set Holly towards the first brushwood fence and raced at it. They cleared it easily. Holly's hooves thudded to the ground and charged on, kicking up divots as she went. The parallel bars, raised higher than the twins had ever seen them, were no problem; Holly was over them and galloping on.

'Come on, Polly!' Linda Moone's voice rose above the others as her daughter flew over the water-jump. 'Oh, good girl!'

'You can do it!' Richard Moone yelled. 'Twenty seconds left. Go for it!'

Holly thundered by, head thrust forward, ears pricked towards the next jump: a tricky treble. Over one, then two, then three. Her heels clicked the last pole. It rattled. The audience gasped, but the pole stayed in place. 'Aah!' The spectators heaved a sigh of relief.

'Go on, Holly!' Hannah yelled.

'Polly, you're nearly there!' called Helen. Caught up in the moment, the twins had briefly forgotten the bad news they'd brought with them.

A high wall stood between Holly and victory. The powerful chestnut ran at it full pelt, adjusted her stride, launched herself through the air.

Hannah closed her eyes to the sound of her dad's

camera clicking and whirring. Helen gripped the fence in front of her.

'A clear round!' the steward cried. 'In sixty-one seconds!'

The cheer that went up drowned out the sound of his voice.

'She did it!' Linda Moone turned to hug her husband. Spotting the Moores standing close by, she rushed across. 'Did you see them?' she gasped. 'Weren't they wonderful? Isn't this just the best day ever?'

Polly stood with Holly beside the trailer that would take her and Solo home to Doveton. Holly's head was up, a red rosette fluttering proudly on her bridle to match Solo's blue one. 'Good girl!' Polly told her over and over. 'I'm so proud of you. You were brilliant!'

As the crowd dispersed for lunch, going off for sandwiches in the refreshment tent, David Moore had quietly taken Richard and Linda Moone to one side.

'Tell her!' Hannah whispered to Helen. She gave her a small push forward, willing her to do it.

'Tell me what?' Polly's face was flushed, her grey eyes bright and shining. She'd just taken off her hard hat and shaken down her long, dark hair. Nothing, it

seemed, could dent her delight.

Helen cleared her throat. 'We've got some bad news.'

'Well, go on, what is it? It can't be that bad.' Stooping to grab hold of a strap under Holly's heaving girth, Polly brought it up and fastened the light rug that would help get her dry and cool. She'd finished the job before Helen could bring herself to utter another word.

'It is,' Hannah muttered uncomfortably. 'It's much worse than you think.' Once more she nudged Helen to go on.

'It's about Star,' Helen said in the faintest voice,

hardly able to breathe.

Polly gasped and went rigid. 'She's not sick!'

'No,' Helen said quickly. 'Not that. But, the fact is, Star's gone missing!'

Hannah saw their new friend's face turn ghostly white. The smile vanished from her eyes and mouth. 'It's true,' she said quietly. 'This sounds awful, Polly, but we think Star's been stolen!'

Nine

While Linda Moone pulled out of the afternoon competition and headed straight for home with Richard and Polly, Helen and Hannah joined their dad to follow straight after.

It was a gloomy journey over Hardstone Pass, where the clouds had gathered and turned heavy and dark. No one spoke, but the twins ran over and over in their minds the events of the day. They remembered the high hopes and taut nerves of the morning, the joy of Solo's and Holly's successes, the sudden, sickening drop into panic when they'd seen Star's stable door swinging open.

'What about this Laura thing?' Hannah whispered

to Helen as David pulled up alongside the Moones' trailer in the stableyard at Manor Farm. 'Should we mention it?'

Quickly Helen shook her head. She told herself that they had to be calm and sensible. 'No. As Dad said, we should try to stick to the exact facts as we know them.'

Hannah got out of the car with a frown. 'So we just drop it?' Easier said than done. Her uncomfortable suspicions about Laura's part in the foal's disappearance wouldn't just melt away.

'I never said that!' Helen replied sharply. 'I just said we don't mention it right now!'

'Stop whispering, you two,' their dad ordered as he closed the car door. 'Let's go and see what we can do to help.'

So they went to join the Moones and, while David offered to lead Solo out of the horse-box, Helen and Hannah carried out the tack. They were within earshot of an earnest conversation going on in the yard.

'Do we call the police?' Linda stood with her husband considering the possibilities. 'Or do we mount a search party to find Star ourselves?' She too had checked the stable inside and out and had found no clues as to what might have happened.

'Hannah thinks Star's been stolen!' Polly reminded them. Until now, she'd stayed pale and quiet. 'That means we should definitely call the police!'

'Not yet.' Like David Moore, Richard Moone wanted to check the facts. He called the twins over to explain one more time, but as they trudged across the yard, they saw Cookson the builder drive up with another man.

They stopped to let the white van pass, noticing that the two men inside looked alike; though one was middle-aged and one was young. What little hair they had was cut short, and they wore black T-shirts which showed their hairy, muscular arms. With their close view of the men, Hannah and Helen judged that they must be father and son.

'About time!' Mr Moone called, his attention suddenly diverted. He tapped his watch and went to give the guilty-looking workmen a good telling off for being late.

Then the mobile phone in Mrs Moone's pocket started to ring. Exasperated by the lack of action, Polly stormed off into the horse-box to fetch Holly.

'. . . Yes, William, hello!' Linda spoke loudly across a bad connection, then listened hard with a frown on her face. 'Tomorrow?' she said. Then: 'That's sooner than we expected . . . yes, OK. Tomorrow around midday. See you then.'

Slipping the phone back into her pocket, the frown deepened. She waited until Richard had finished giving the Cooksons their instructions, then passed on the latest news. 'That was William Baxter,' she called. 'He's arrived home a few days early, so he plans to call in and see Lady Jane and Star tomorrow lunchtime!'

Straight away Polly reappeared on the ramp. 'Mum, call the police!' she insisted, her round face screwed up with worry. 'What are we waiting for? If Mr Baxter turns up and finds his horse missing, what are we going to do?'

Linda turned to David, who by now had saddled Solo and was fastening the girth. 'What do you think?'

He shot an apologetic look at Polly and the twins. 'I wouldn't want to set up a wild goose chase involving the police,' he said quietly. 'If it turns out that the foal simply got out, that is.'

'You think we should take another look for ourselves – just in case the door was left open by mistake?' Linda thrust her hands in her pockets and let her gaze range over the landscape, resting at last on the high fells in the distance. 'Let's hope that if Star did get out, she didn't go too far,' she murmured.

As she and David talked, Richard Moone came up. 'David's right,' he commented briskly. 'Leave the police out of it until this evening at least. Meanwhile, I'll ring round the local farms to ask if anyone's seen the foal.' He headed straight inside the house to carry out the task.

'And I'll drive round the lanes,' Linda decided, making for her car which was parked round the front of the house. 'With any luck, I'll be able to pick up a few clues.'

'Me too.' David handed Solo's reins to Helen, then joined in with this part of the plan. He told the twins that he would see them up at Home Farm by teatime, when hopefully there would be good news about the missing youngster.

'Polly?' Left in the emptying yard, with the sound of the builders' sharp picks beginning to hack into the concrete surface, Hannah turned to the figure still standing on the horse-box ramp. 'What do you want to do?'

'We've got twenty-four hours to find her!' she whispered in a strained voice.

'Less,' Helen pointed out. 'Star will get hungry by

teatime today. If she's out on the fell and has to stay there all night, she'll get really cold.'

'She could starve or freeze!' Polly's head dropped and she hid her face in her hands.

'So?' Hannah demanded. It was more than she could do to stay here talking. She needed to be out there looking with the others. 'Are you coming to help us, or not?'

Polly rubbed her eyes and looked up angrily. 'This is all your fault!' she accused Helen angrily.

'Polly!' Hannah took a step forward to defend her sister, then faltered.

Helen's eyes widened at the sudden accusation. It left her speechless and unable to defend herself because deep down, despite their robbery theory, she still feared it might be true.

'If Star wasn't stolen and did get out like Mum seems to think, that must mean you let her!' By now Polly was so upset she flung blame everywhere. 'If it hadn't been for you two forgetting to make sure that the door was shut, none of this would have happened!'

Helen and Hannah left Polly without a word in their own defence.

'She's all mixed up!' Hannah muttered as she rode

Solo down the bridleway to the pebbled shore.

'Me too,' Helen admitted miserably.

'Yes, but don't take any notice of Polly.' Hannah knew that if they did, they wouldn't be able to concentrate on the task of finding clues to the mystery surrounding Star.

For a while they went on in silence. By the time they reached the lakeside, the dark clouds of Rydal Fell had begun to produce big, cold spots of rain. They pock-marked the smooth, grey surface of the water, and made black splodges on the grey pebbles.

'What exactly are we looking for?' Helen said at last. She'd peered over walls and under hedges, stood on rocks to get a better view of the beach, but she'd spotted nothing unusual.

Hannah shrugged and turned in the saddle. Up the hill, beyond Manor Farm and the larger, grander outline of Doveton Manor, she could make out their dad's car slowly winding its way up the narrow road to Home Farm. 'We're looking for a clue,' she insisted, turning back to the shore. 'Any clue!'

'Or anyone who might have been around at the time and seen what happened,' Helen suggested. Her gaze swept along the dreary, empty beach.

'Right, that's it!' Hannah reined Solo back then

jumped down from the saddle. She faced Helen, eyeball to eyeball. 'If you won't say it, I will!'

'W-what?' Helen knew it was unusual for Hannah to raise her voice like this.

'We're wasting our time here!' Her brown eyes blazed. 'This isn't where we should be looking!'

'W-where then?' The cold drops splashed on her hot face, a strong wind tugged at her hair as Hannah pointed across the beach.

'At Doveton Manor, that's where!' She even made Solo jump and skitter sideways in her excitement. 'Come on, Helen, let's go and find out what Laura Saunders knows about all this!'

'What if we're wrong?' Helen muttered.

They'd tethered Solo to the paddock fence and crunched up the gravel drive to the grandest house in the village. Stone angels stood by the fishpond, staring at them with blind eyes. Lady, the Siamese cat, watched from the comfort of the warm, dry summer house.

'You want to turn back?' Hannah challenged, her jaw set, her hands clenched as she approached the stableyard by the side of the house.

Helen frowned. 'No!' Hannah was right, she

decided. They had to confront Laura. But her heart was in her mouth all the same.

Hannah marched straight to Sultan's stable and peered inside. She saw the handsome chestnut horse contentedly munching hay from a net which hung from the whitewashed wall. But no Laura.

'Try the tack-room,' Helen suggested faintly. The sooner they got this over, the better.

As Hannah went to knock and wait, Sultan poked his head over his door. He gave a loud, high neigh.

Helen paused mid-stride. 'What is it?' she asked him. But she had no time to find out before a tall, slim figure in blue jodphurs and a cream sweater joined him at the door. 'Hannah!' Helen called. 'Laura's over here!'

'What do you want?' Laura brushed hay from her sweater. Her eyes were hooded and suspicious, her voice nastily abrupt.

To Hannah it seemed certain that Laura had known they were there all along. She guessed that there was no point beating about the bush. 'Star's vanished,' she said. 'We wanted to ask you if you've seen her.'

'Who's Star when she's at home?' Laura sneered, precisely picking a last wisp of hay from her jumper.

'Hmm.' Hannah grunted. Laura was playing dumb.

Even if she and Polly were worst enemies, Doveton was such a small place that the Saunders would be bound to have heard about the surprise birth of Lady Jane's blue roan foal. 'Come on, Laura, do you know anything? If you do, just tell us, please!'

Helen let Hannah do the talking. Meanwhile, she studied Laura's face.

'You must be joking!' she retorted, her fair complexion colouring up. 'But, as a matter of fact, it's not funny. You're standing there practically accusing me of hiding vital evidence about some pathetic missing horse!'

Flinging open Sultan's door, she stormed towards Hannah. 'Well, just get out!' she cried, her ponytail swinging across her face as she turned from one to the other. 'Go on, both of you; get out!'

'Not until you tell us.' Helen stepped across her path, speaking up at last. Laura's hasty, over-the-top reaction had convinced her that she did have something to hide.

'Tell you what?' Laura yelled, almost spitting with anger. Then she turned and stormed off towards the corner of the big stone house, stopping only for one last angry volley at Hannah and Helen, who stared after her.

'And stop looking at me like that!' she flung over her shoulder. 'Go and look for Polly Moone's precious horse, but don't drag me in. I don't know anything about Star going missing – not a single thing – a big fat nought, OK!'

Ten

'Well, I don't believe her!' Helen stomped up the lane to Home Farm wearing an expression of disgust.

'Me neither.' Hannah agreed that Laura was hiding something, but had to face the fact that they'd come up against a brick wall. Now she just wanted to get Solo safely home and to find out if their dad had found any clues of his own about how and why Star had disappeared. It was almost teatime; the rain was still coming down steadily and making them more miserable than ever.

'Why is she behaving like this?' Helen couldn't let the subject of Laura drop. Brushing a rain droplet from the end of her nose, she held open the gate for

Hannah and Solo. 'I'd never have thought she could be so horrible!'

Hannah walked Solo to the barn door then dismounted. 'Guilty conscience!' she said darkly.

'Meaning, she knows what happened to Star but won't say?' Helen nodded and moved in close to whisper her idea. 'Listen, Hann, I vote we sneak back to the Manor before it gets dark and search the stables!'

'You think Laura's actually hiding Star there?'

Helen nodded again. 'That's exactly what I think! She knows how much Star must mean to Polly, so she just took the foal out of spite, without stopping to think.'

'She wouldn't!' Hannah gasped. 'It would be too risky, for a start!'

'Yeah, but she was probably desperate,' Helen pointed out as they untacked Solo and hung up his bridle and saddle. 'People do stupid things to cover up. Laura knows she did something really bad, but now she can't get out of it. So she has to hide Star at Doveton Manor and hope that no one suspects her . . .' Thoughtfully she led the way across the yard, stooping to pat Speckle who had raced out of the house to greet her.

Just then, their dad appeared at the door. 'There's a phone call for you!' He passed on the message with a puzzled frown.

'Who for? Me or Helen?' Hannah asked.

'Either.' David stood to one side to let them through.

'Who from?'

'Laura,' he told them with a quizzical shrug. Then; 'Get a move on. She says it's urgent!'

'Hannah?' Laura's quivering voice spoke faintly down the phone.

'No, it's Helen. What do you want?' *What cheek!* she thought. *She rings us up to tell us another lie. Well, she needn't think she's getting away with it!*

'Helen, listen. I'm sorry!'

Taken aback, she held the phone away from her ear.

'Are you still there? I'm sorry, OK?'

Helen sniffed. 'What about?'

'For being so . . . whatever . . . you know . . . about Polly Moone.' Laura fumbled for words. Then she gathered speed. 'I don't know what came over me these last couple of weeks. And listen, I really am sorry about her foal going missing . . . and for lying to you when you asked me about it.'

111

Once more, Helen pulled the phone away. 'Laura's admitting it!' she hissed at Hannah.

'. . . I did know about it, because Mrs Moone had already called in to tell me. I lied to her too.' Laura fell silent, obviously struggling with tears.

'You've got Star in your stables, haven't you?' Helen demanded.

'No!' The shocked voice replied quickly. 'No, honestly, Helen, I haven't!'

'You stole her!'

'No! I don't blame you for thinking that, since I've been such a pig to you lately. The truth is, I was jealous because you made friends with Polly. But I didn't steal Star, you must believe me!' Laura pleaded. 'What I lied about was the fact that I hadn't seen her!'

'So you did?' Helen followed the zig-zags of Laura's confession.

'Yes. I took Sultan up the fell after we got back from Nesfield. I needed to get away for a while, you know. So, anyway, we rode up your lane and took a short cut past Crackpot Farm. That's where I saw the foal!'

Helen gasped. 'By herself? What was she doing there? Why didn't you stop her?'

'Hang on a second. I didn't do anything about it, OK?' Laura's voice grew fainter again. 'I know I should've, but I didn't. So I'm doing it now. I'm coming up to look!'

'Where exactly?' Events were racing on so fast that Helen could hardly catch her breath.

'To the Lawsons' place. See you there!' Laura put down the phone and the line went dead.

Crackpot Farm was shut up for the weekend. The doors were closed, the car missing from the yard.

'Please let Laura be telling the truth!' Hannah muttered as she let Speckle off the lead.

The Border collie cocked his head to one side and gazed up at her, waiting to be told what to do.

'Here, Speckle!' Helen called him to the barn and set him sniffing at the wide, wooden door. His sharp nose snuffled at the narrow gap beneath it, while Helen tried the handle. 'Locked!' she called to Hannah. 'There's no way Star could have got in here!'

Hannah gazed round the yard. She crept close to the sturdy hutch that stood under the Lawsons' kitchen window and peered through the chicken-wire door. Sorrel, Sam's silky black rabbit, twitched her long ears and wrinkled her nose back at her. 'If only you could talk!' Hannah whispered. 'You'd tell us where Star has got to!'

'Not here!' Helen said in a hollow voice as she wandered back without Speckle. The dog's nose had taken him off round the back of the barn. 'But here comes Laura!'

Hannah straightened up to see a figure pedalling along the rough farm track. Laura wore a blue anorak, hood up against the rain, which she pushed back as she dropped the bike and ran to meet them.

'Did you find her?' she gasped.

Hannah and Helen shook their heads warily. Perhaps this was all still a big con on Laura's part.

'Did you try the field at the back?' she demanded, ignoring their suspicious and immediately heading that way.

'Speckle's there . . .' Helen began. A loud bark confirmed this; a sign perhaps that their dog had discovered a clue. She and Hannah sped after Laura.

'This was where I saw the foal!' Laura ran round the barn and showed them a sloping, uneven field full of sheep and lambs. 'I was quite a long way off, but even so, I'm sure I wasn't mistaken!'

'Well, she's not here now!' Hannah couldn't hide her disappointment. A dozen or more white lambs jumped and frolicked over the damp tussocks, carefully watched by their mothers. But there was no tiny grey foal taking shelter under a bush or drinking from the stream that tumbled across the field.

It was another bark from Speckle which drew them back towards the barn. There was a rough lean-to shed at one corner. The corrugated-iron roof was rusty, a plastic sheet flapping across its entrance. It seemed damp and dismal; most likely a store for old machinery or timber.

'What is it, Speckle?' Laura dropped on to one knee to peer through the torn and ragged plastic sheet. Rain spattered loudly against it as Helen and Hannah joined her and she pulled it slowly to one side.

The shed was dark and full of cobwebs. There was a pile of old logs giving off a musty smell and a collapsed bale of straw in one corner. And something shifting in the pale straw, making it rustle . . . an animal with large, dark eyes and a bony head, with a clear white star on its forehead.

'Poor little thing!' Helen held herself back from smothering Star with hugs. She saw how the foal trembled and tried to stand on her weak legs, how they folded underneath her as she sank down into the straw. 'She's exhausted!'

'And hungry!' Hannah whispered.

'How are we going to get her back to Manor Farm?' Helen wondered. She eased forward to comfort the frightened foal.

The question was answered by the sound of a car splashing through the puddles in the farmyard. It pulled up and doors slammed.

Hannah turned to Laura. 'Who can that be?'

'The Moones,' she answered quietly. 'I rang them before I came up, told them the whole story. They said they'd get here as soon as they could.'

So, as Helen coaxed Star to her feet with soft, encouraging words, Laura ran to fetch Linda and Richard Moone. They came prepared, with a blanket and bottle; relief was written all over their faces.

'Here, Helen.' Linda Moone handed over the milk feed. 'Go easy; don't let her gulp it down too quickly.'

'Don't worry, Helen's done it loads of times before,' Hannah told her. She felt her whole body relax as Helen laid the blanket over Star's back, then settled in the straw beside her, one arm around her neck, the other holding the bottle steady as the foal sucked. Head back, with milk dribbling down her chin, Star closed her eyes and drank her fill.

* * *

'And so the mystery of how Star vanished may never be solved!' David Moore told the twins' mum. It was late the same night and everyone was safely home.

'But she's back where she belongs, that's what matters.' Mary sighed contentedly, her feet up on the warm kitchen stove, a mug of tea made by the twins balanced in her lap.

'Laura's off the hook . . . we think!' David winked at Helen and Hannah. 'For a time she came under a heavy cloud of suspicion. But she turned out to be the hero in the end!'

'And I take it Polly's happy?' their mum asked.

'Must be, I guess. She proved she was the best rider in the gymkhana, then she got the lost foal back,' David reflected. 'Mind you, by the time I got to Crackpot Farm, it was all over. Richard and Linda were loading the foal into their Land Rover and there was no sign of Polly.'

'That's fine, then!' Mary sighed. She lifted her mug to let Socks creep on to her lap. 'All's well that ends well!'

'Helen?' Hannah whispered across their dark bedroom. The curtains were open, but heavy clouds blocked out the moon and stars. 'Are you awake?'

There was no answer.

'Helen?' She wasn't asleep, Hannah knew. 'Let's go down to Manor Farm first thing tomorrow.'

'What for?' came the slow reply.

'To see Star, of course.'

'Don't know. Maybe.' Helen turned her back and pulled the duvet over her head. 'Go to sleep!' she mumbled.

But she couldn't take her own advice. A whole hour later she was still wide awake. It was all right for Hannah; she wasn't the one who'd bolted Star's door. It wasn't Hannah whom everyone still secretly blamed!

By Sunday morning the sky had cleared. The yard at Manor Farm lay in puddles after the rain, but the Cooksons were already hard at work on the drains by the time the twins showed up at nine-thirty.

Hannah ran eagerly past the workmen to the stable where the foal had spent the night. She saw Polly mucking out and sprinted to join her. 'How's Star?' she cried.

Helen hung back, wondering why she'd agreed to come. Her name round here was as muddy as the puddle she'd just stepped in. It was as if a big finger of blame was pointing down from the clear sky, a voice booming 'It's you!'

'. . . Load of fuss about nothing!' the younger builder grumbled. With his back to the girls, waist-deep in the hole they'd dug, he hadn't spotted Helen hanging about at the corner of the yard, or Hannah coming back to fetch her. 'A horse goes missing! What's the big deal?'

Hannah stopped and frowned. She stepped into the shadow of the pool conversion to listen.

The older man also stopped work. 'This type makes a fuss all the time. They move out here and start lording it over us locals; do this, do that. The drain isn't good enough, do it again, rabbit-rabbit-rabbit!'

Cookson junior laughed slyly. 'Don't let Moone catch you talking that like.'

'So? He thinks he's Mr big-shot estate agent, but where was he yesterday morning when I needed a word with him? So, I was held up, but I got here in the end! Turns out he'd already gone off to some poncey pony show!'

Yesterday morning? Hannah held her breath. Surely the builders hadn't turned up at Manor Farm until the afternoon?

'I drive over specially to see him,' Cookson went

on. 'The place is deserted except for those two twins, and they're busy taking a horse out into the field!'

Hannah's hand flew to her mouth, then she beckoned Helen across.

'I try the house, I try every blinking stable, looking for Moone. Can I find him? No way!'

'It was *you*!' Hannah couldn't stay quiet any longer. She jumped out of the shadows and flew towards them. Across the yard, Polly heard the disturbance and stepped out of Star's stable.

'*You* left Star's door open!' Hannah cried, eyes blazing, standing hands on hips over the men in the hole. 'And you let my sister take the blame!'

'That's enough surprises for one weekend!' Linda Moone had let Richard deal with the careless builders while she and Polly thanked the twins for uncovering the truth.

'I agree!' Polly beamed. 'But thanks, Hannah. Thanks, Helen. If you, Speckle and Laura hadn't found Star, I'm sure she'd have died!'

'That's OK!' Helen blushed and smiled back. She was leading Star down to the bottom field, where Lady Jane stood at the wall waiting for her runaway foal.

'What we need is a nice, quiet morning before

William Baxter arrives.' Linda opened the gate. 'A chance for us all to get over the excitement of the last twenty-four hours!'

The grey mare came calmly towards Star, nudging her gently while Helen took off the headcollar. Star stood, legs splayed, shaking her head. Then, once free, she gave a skip and a jump across the flower-covered field.

'Nothing wrong with her that a good feed and a rest didn't put right!' Mrs Moone said, happy at last.

Nodding, Helen and Hannah backed out of the field. And there, coming down the bridleway, as if by chance, but not fooling anybody, was Laura.

'Hi!' She darted shy glances at the twins and Polly. 'I saw you out here and wondered . . . well . . . if you'd fancy meeting up for a ride later?'

'You bet!' Hannah jumped in. 'When? Where?'

'Bags I ride Solo first!' Helen grinned at Hannah.

'Typical!' Hannah grinned back.

'How about you?' Laura turned nervously to Polly. 'Would you like to come?'

The twins kept on smiling. *At last. About time. Brilliant!*

Polly's rosebud mouth twitched. Her eyes sparkled. 'Course I would,' she replied. 'I've wanted to go with you and Sultan for weeks . . . I thought you'd never ask!'

HOME FARM TWINS
Jenny Oldfield

66127 5	Speckle The Stray	£3.99	❏
66128 3	Sinbad The Runaway	£3.99	❏
66129 1	Solo The Homeless	£3.99	❏
66130 5	Susie The Orphan	£3.99	✓
66131 3	Spike The Tramp	£3.99	❏
66132 1	Snip and Snap The Truants	£3.99	❏
68990 0	Sunny The Hero	£3.99	❏
68991 9	Socks The Survivor	£3.99	❏
68992 7	Stevie The Rebel	£3.99	❏
68993 5	Samson The Giant	£3.99	❏
69983 3	Sultan The Patient	£3.99	❏
69984 1	Sorrel The Substitute	£3.99	❏
69985 X	Skye The Champion	£3.99	❏
69986 8	Sugar and Spice The Pickpockets	£3.99	❏
69987 6	Sophie The Show-off	£3.99	❏
72682 2	Smoky The Mystery	£3.99	❏
72795 0	Scott The Braveheart	£3.99	❏
72796 9	Spot The Prisoner	£3.99	❏